AF455146

# S.O.C.K.

## THE SCHOOL
OF THE
## *CLOAKED KNIFE*

GARRY TURNER

This is a work of fiction. Names, faces, characters, places and incidents are either the product of the author's imagination or are used fictitiously, and any resemblance to actual people, living or dead, business establishments, events or locales is entirely coincidental.

Published by Lulu
Copyright 2011 Garry Turner
All Rights Reserved

ISBN 978-1-257-77612-2

Written By: Garry Turner
Editing and Final Reading: Rosina Tassone Turner
Graphic Design & Layout:
Mark Pye www.designsthatcaptivate.com

## *Acknowledgements*

Like to give thanks to the genius of Ian Fleming and all the "James Bond" trademark stories and movies. They kept my mind afloat as a young boy imagining the fancy cars with machine guns and exploding pens.

Like to give thanks to the memory of Felix Dzerzhinsky. He was a true spy and the real inspiration for this book.

Like to give thanks to the Prince George Public Library for their resources while creating this Spy Series.

Like to give thanks to My Mother who has always taught me to delve inside the deepest part of my mind. Her wonderful energy has given me the wonderful life that I have.

**This book is for**
**My Son Damien**

*As the night falls into darkness, the children of the world sleep safely…*

*The children have a new hero, a new savior from the dark corners of the world…*

*S.O.C.K.*

# THE SCHOOL OF THE CLOAKED KNIFE

# CONTENTS

# THE SCHOOL OF THE *CLOAKED KNIFE*

## CHAPTER 1

The sweat beaded on the Captains face as his stern brow gave him the look of a person who was held prisoner from his own thoughts. The enigma was clattering away with a message from Deutschland.

The crew of Uboat-1301 whispered back and forth. The entire U-boat was on edge. The message coming through was the new orders. The new orders would divulge their new location and they all wondered what the encrypted message would say.

"Kapitän!" the enigma operator motioned for the captain to come over.

The captain of the U-boat made his way over to the enigma through the bodies around him. Looking at the lamp panel the operator watched as the first rotor rolled forward it started to advance on the twenty six letter combination moving forward to stop on letter "B". The next rotor moved stopping on the letter "H".

The operator wrote these two letters down in the logbook in front of him. He waited for the next rotor to turn. It stopped on the letter "D" pause for a second then the next and last rotor moved to the position "G".

This was the starting point of their location he would have to type this code back to the Third Reich in order for the code to be encrypted.

Each rotor had the capability of 26 different

positions and gave the message 456,976 possibilities.

"Kapitän!" The newest location is here."

The captain was at the chart now waiting for the orders to be coded. The sweat was pouring down the Captain's forehead now as the numbers where read to him. The sweat rolled past his eyebrows and into his left eye, he swept it away with his hand and began to work out the co-ordinates on the map.

"The Black Sea longitude."

"Latitude."

"Sending Back."

The Captain nodded as the young enigma operator pushed the first button. The rotor moved forward to the first letter combination, he stopped in on "D". Relaying back the original message the operator pushed the rest of the rotors to the appropriate positions. The radar operator was the youngest of the crew and he was a mere 17 years old. He now pushed the button for the sounding radar contact.

"They have not yet detected us Kapitän!" He spoke.

The alarm was now sounding the red lights flashing as everything went dark inside the U-boat.

"Kapitän!"

"Starboard 60 knots, down the bell angle 500 meters, there is the sound of Star Class Japanese Submarine." The radar operator spoke.

"Resume main course!" the Captain whispered.

The submarine was on silent run, everyone inside the capsule held even their breath at this point only exhaling when they had to. The captain motioned cutting the air with his hand to signal to the alarm to be turned off.

"We must elude them." The captain whispered again.

Take her down another 500 meters to 1200." The captain was of High Blood and would not falter under any circumstances.

"We now sit and wait." The captain whispered his orders.

"All engines stop." The captain's voice was echoed down the line.

"All engines stop."

# THE SCHOOL OF THE CLOAKED KNIFE

## CHAPTER 2

Twelve-year old Stanton paused for a moment the suspense of the story was killing him. The book he held in his hand was a gift from his Father who had put it under his pillow one day.

The U-boat being under attack had made him turn the page the next chapter beginning. He continued to read as fast as his mind could see the words. Whispering under his breath he turned the next page his hands shaking with excitement.

Stanton was stuck at the summer cottage while his parents where on vacation. Miss Sheldon his caregiver was there to take care of him. She was in the kitchen taking out a newly plucked chicken from a water bin and proceeded to stuff the skin with butter, rubbing salt onto the skin to make it crispy and the meat underneath juicy.

Vladivostok was the city on the edge of Asia. It was the place of mystery for Stanton and his family had just moved here before the summer. He did not have a clue on how to speak Russian and they where some distance from anyone. So being stuck at the cabin had at least turned not so boring with the book he had in his hand. The book had a bit of German and he was learning a few words while he read. The summer breeze swept in from the door, the sea air carrying the salty smell of seaweed.

"You mind your manners while your parents are gone young man," Miss Sheldon voice rose above the running tap.

"I am not going to be able to look after you night and day." Miss Sheldon's voice was of suspicion.

She poured some milk and laid a few cookies on a plate.

"But that doesn't mean you have to starve!" Miss Sheldon said smiling she patted his auburn hair making him wipe it back down to its original position.

Crunching a cookie he took a big sip of the milk, it was ice cold from the icebox. The iceman had delivered it just that day so the milk was at its coldest temperature. Wiping the wetness from his top lip with the back of his hand Stanton grabbed the last two remaining cookies stood up and then went to walk to the back door.

"Mind yourself outside don't go drowning yourself in the ocean, Ok Dear!" Miss Sheldon smiled and returned to making dinner. The door opened to the sound of seagulls and the crashing of the ocean. His footsteps could be heard as he pounded down the stairs.

"One, Two, Three, Four, 1 and a 2 and a 3 and a 4 and a."

He sang as he jumped down the steps and leaped off them to the ground.

He starts walking towards the paved path that led either to the carport or down to the sandy beach. He picked the path that led to the beach deciding to go that way. The paved path was a zigzag that led past a parking lot. The path stopped as soon as it reached the white crystal sand. Now a long beach ran out from the surf from which was now at high tide and crashed against the shore some distance away. It was quite breezy here along this part of the shore and once he had been given a kite of magnificent size. It was a box kite his Father had brought him back from his trip to Canada. It roared high above the surf until one day he had let it out way to far just like his Father had warned him not to. The wind picked up quickly and ripped at the rope in his hand there was not enough rope left on the spool to hold the giant box kite and it ripped it free. It was like watching a huge bird being let go for the first time Stanton thought. His boyish smile led him to laughter as he started running after the kite. Yelling to it in what few words of Russian he new at this point. "Free, Free."

# THE SCHOOL OF THE CLOAKED KNIFE

## CHAPTER 3

Stanton ran on the beach following the path of the kite. The kite rose and as it caught the fast air current it just flew out of site and disappeared. He had felt such joy for the kite to fly free that he did not think of what the consequences could be after letting it go.

Stanton was not laughing so hard when his father found out that the kite had flown away. There was quite to do about getting things given to him and keeping care not to lose them or break them or else there was to be no more kites or anything.

He had put that past his mind till now but Stanton still smiled as he looked up in the sky and saw the kite that set itself free in his mind. He stood for a moment at the end of the path and traced the sky with his finger watching the clouds move in front of his gaze.

Taking his shoes off he was now barefoot and ready to tackle the long hike down the beach to the end of the bay. Maybe there will be new ships today he thought. There is always a barge to look at though. Leaping from the pavement his feet landed in the very warm sand heated from the sun all day. He dug his toes in under the hot sand to a cooler under layer of sand. The sand being heated by the sun all day had made it almost unbearable for Stanton to walk on. Moving along the sandy beach now Stanton scoped out anything his eye could find like any little boy would do in the world, even a rock was a special thing to look at. Sometimes Stanton would sit and watch the boats move into the harbor. He crossed the beach walking along the shoreline the cold water rushing over his feet as he made tracks in the sand. They would disappear in minutes as the tide flowed in and out his foot impressions just a memory. There was a spot on the beach where it's sandy tongue jutted out into the ocean. It was well protected from the surf by a gigantic rock that lay strewn on the side of the sandy spike that Stanton now walked to. He liked to sit on this really big flat rock that was big enough for him to lie on his back flat. It was on a slight angle, just the right angle to sit and stare out into the ocean and the sky. He had to climb down a couple of other rocks to get to the rock that he liked. They where a bit slippery today and he lost his footing once making his heart race he managed to get his balance and leaped to the next rock. Stanton still had the book in his hand as he then sat down and opened it. He found the page that he had bent over in the corner holding his place.

"Now where was I? Oh Ya." He said aloud.

Stanton pawed through the book looking for the chapter he was on as he laid his back flat on the rock and continued to read the next chapter of his book. No sooner had he started reading Stanton heard voices coming from behind him. The voices started coming closer and closer, his heart started to pound. Stanton did not like strangers very much and he was going to make sure not to be seen. Not letting his head stick above the rocks he rolled onto his stomach to peer the top. He saw five boys, two looking of about 16 he thought. Being 16 was a big number for Stanton. That is when boys started getting their drivers licenses, girl friends and staying out later. Stanton had just started to wait for that time in anticipation. He looked at the other two boys, they where his age for sure. The fifth one with the glasses was definitely his age he thought. The voices of the boys where coming very close now. Close enough for him to start to hear what they where saying.

# THE SCHOOL OF THE CLOAKED KNIFE

# CHAPTER 4

One spoke in Russian, saying something in a very hurried rushed voice rising at the end like he was very agitated. The second boy spoke in English.

"What do you expect from them, I have seen them take away children before." his rich Russian accent was funny to Stanton he almost laughed out loud.

"There is the Resistance we must not forget, we do not forget about them." the fourth boy said with the same accent as the second boy.

The boy's voices were now drifting away as they walked past where Stanton lay.

The fifth boy spoke Russian once again in agitation,

"We are going to be there soon, Carscov will have our hides if you do not get to the School on time." the oldest one said.

"School?" Stanton wondered

There were no schools in this part of Vladovostok.

They where far enough down the beach now, that the boys voices where to far to hear.

The curiosity got the best of him so he slipped his shoes on. Not before untying the knot that he made for a test.

Grabbing a small rock he hid his book in the crevice below it``113.

"I will come back for it." he thought.

Stanton kept as far back as possible trying not to

look too obvious, like a cat he crept behind the group of five boys. They kept walking around the coastline and then past his house. He never went this way, it just led up to a Lighthouse atop a high wall of rock.

It was impassable the beach just ended at the bottom of it, the surf hitting the giant columns of rock that jutted from the sea.

He hid behind just a small amount of bushes that grew against the shallow wall that formed out of the sand.

He was sure they did not hear him or see him because they continued to walk and talk, but they did look behind them once scanning behind to make sure no one was following them.

They came up to the rock in a particular spot there was a root sticking out of the side of the wall, it was visible now to Stanton because the first boy climbed up part way up the wall using it as a foot hold.

"I'll be back in a moment." the first boy said to the others.

There were other roots that led up the wall and the boy proceeded to use these as his footholds to climb the wall.

He disappeared up the wall and over onto a ledge that was not visible from the ground but once the boy climbed onto it, Stanton could see there was a plateau to stand on.

There was the sound of grinding rocks, as a small hidden door was now visible at the base of the giant rock wall.

The first boy climbed down the roots just after a few moments of his absence.

There was some laughter as they all entered the now visible opening in the rock.

Stanton thought

"There is no time to get to that opening before it closes."

He was right the wall closed behind the boys as fast as they moved past it.

"ScreeEEech!"

The door now was completely invisible to the naked eye.

There was nothing to discern whether or not a door ever actually existed.

He crept up to the wall, looking at the root that the boy used to climb up.

# THE SCHOOL OF THE CLOAKED KNIFE

# CHAPTER 5

“He must have opened it from up there” Stanton surmised.

The root was a bit too high for him but with the determination of a 12 year old boy, he managed to clamber up onto the foothold’ Scraping his knee several times in the attempt.

He was bleeding and scarred but with triumph he started to climb to the next root.

The ground was getting further away now and he did not dare look down, he just kept climbing until he came to the ledge.

This was the tricky part, he had to hoist himself over onto the ledge.

Faltering a little he managed to get his body onto the ledge. Swinging one foot over and then pulling himself up onto the ledge, he was able to get the other leg over.

He was now standing and looking onto the sea.

“How wonderful”

He thought this is great, I would have never known this was here.

Searching his surroundings, there didn’t seem to be anything here, just a ledge, some dirt and rocks.

“Ah, the rocks.”

Stanton look around the rocks by the wall, there was one particular rock that looked out of place it was black as the night and was very jagged. He could see an object on the ground just beside it.

He picked it up, somehow it was very light.

Dropping it into the impression in the ground, a click sounded.

“That’s it, what a strange way to keep a door locked” he thought.

“Now to the task of climbing down!”

His stomach ached now he did not like heights very much.

He managed to get to the ground with a few more cuts but this time on the lower part of his calf on the left leg. He just wiped the blood away with the dirt and dropped to the ground, his feet digging into the sand filling his shoes.

Taking them off he proceeded to dump them out.

The door was closing fast and he leaped through it landing straight on his belly the dirt filling his mouth.

His one shoe still in his hand. The door closed leaving, him almost in complete darkness.

It took a second for his eyes to adjust but there was a small glimmer of light from holes in the rock from above.

A torchlight could be seen in the distance some ways to the west of where Stanton was.

He thought of his Mother and Father just then, they

where off on some tropical island, he did not ask them this time for it was just another trip to him.

“How could I be here, I should leave.” Stanton thought to himself.

Pressing on toward the torch light he could now hear voices from a distance. He crept up to the entrance to the next passage, he saw many boys and girls his age, some younger and even some older. They walked in single file and they where wearing black uniforms, a patch of some kind with an emblem on it. They marched very silently surprisingly to him there were so many of them. He ducked back into the darkness as they passed. The uniformed boys continued to march in single file down the long corridor without noticing him so he crept out into the hallway to follow them.

His 12 year-old fears out weighed his 12-year-old curiosity. Stanton’s knees shook a little as he walked but he managed to not make to much noise. The corridor broke into a giant room, there where more boys in uniforms starting to form lines and get into order.

# THE SCHOOL
# OF THE
# *CLOAKED KNIFE*

## CHAPTER 6

He could see the five boys that he had followed from the beach, at the side just down from where he was standing, only now they had uniforms on but kept their hats in their hands.

Soon there was order and everyone was now facing the podium and stage that was before these boys and girls.

Tap Tap Tap, from the podium,

The rustling in the room started to quiet down.

Tap Tap Tap

There was silence in the room now and all the boys and girls where at attention staring towards the figure who rose from his seat beside the podium.

Raising his long bony hands, the man spoke in English with a Russian accent.

"Welcome all, welcome comrades!"

"This new year will bring many great deeds for us to challenge ourselves with."

"There are many who need our help, you must train and learn, each of you will learn to achieve new levels this year."

The masses all turned and cheered to each other clasping each other on the back

"Quiet, comrades plenty of time to revel in this new challenge."

Whispering next to Stanton a boy said to another boy

slightly younger than Stanton.

"There has not been a higher level for any of us for some time now, It must be a big a mission and it must be someone big who we have to save from their demise."

"You." the bony hand points towards the youngest of the bunch, "Even the youngest will be asked many tasks that will benefit our cause."

"We have a new comer to our midst, a curious mind just like the rest of you, he has happened up on us I am sure without knowing why, come out here young man."

Stanton somehow new he was the one the bony-handed man was talking about.

"That's right boy come, come, did you think you would make it inside our school without being noticed.

"These boys here," pointing to the 5 boys from the beach, "They told me of your presence the moment you crept from your little hiding place amongst those rocks."

The entire congregation of boys and girls looked towards where the schoolmaster had pointed. There was no hiding now, he knew he had to come out of his hiding spot.

The crowd parted so he could walk amongst them towards the School Master and the front of the stage.

"Yes right beside me young man" the bony hand again motioned him to stand to his right.

"Curiosity is a spy's most valued passion." The Head Master spoke. "You cannot know enough about your surroundings or the things in it" he continued "You have caught the curiosity by the tale and you ran with it my boy."

The entire school erupted into laughter. Every kid turned to each other with huge smiles. These smiles where the smiles that came from someone else's torment. There was also the laughter that gains the person being laughed at quick notice amongst a crowd.

"Tell us your name my boy, since you have graciously decided to join our school here we should know your name. It is Stanton Westwood is in not? Well? Speak up my boy."

Stanton thought he heard a bit of Sherlock Holmes in that Russian accent and his mind was racing a thousand miles a minute, "A spy, Me, how could that be."

"Yes sir, Stanton Westood, The Third after my Father and Grandfather."

Stanton did not really understand how the Head Master knew his name but things where moving fast and he was only 12 after all, that was quite over his head at this point.

# THE SCHOOL OF THE CLOAKED KNIFE

# CHAPTER 7

Holding his hands up to the entire school, the headmaster, with great emphasis and knowledge he asked the school,

"Do we add another to the fold lads? – We know there is great need for help we are to do great things, will this boy have the courage and the fortitude. What say yes?" he continued "Let us show in a way of hands, let us vote for his entrance, you decide his fate, for your decision will decide ours."

Stanton beamed as he saw every hand go up, there was not one boy or girl that did not raise their hand it was unanimous.

"So be it, let us move on to other matter, you can go stand at the back young sir, stand by Haritum, he will be your guide."

The headmaster continued on with his sermon, but Stanton did not pay attention his mind was a flutter of ideas. He could not even begin to understand the new world he was just brought himself into. There was a lot to do about school ethics and the code of the school. There was some stuff about the mission that was kept from Stanton but the Headmaster did say that if he continued to learn and grow that his first mission would be a special one. Stanton's mind went to even more ideas of chases in the dark and the dark mystery of being a spy. The headmaster had finished his sermon. A tall boy with a special badge on his shoulder handed the headmaster a file of papers.

The headmaster took out a single sheet of paper. The headmaster handed the sheet to Stanton. On the piece of paper was an enrollment form that read:

**S.O.C.K.**

***In memorandum, I hereby, on this day, to thee swear, that I, Stanton Westwood, by the oath of complete code of silence and honor code, herby do swear by complete code of conduct, forward do thee swear, here and now to uphold the code of school ethics, as per agreed, I will not discuss or diverge what is entitled to me by my rank and level. From here on I am foremost a leader and rank of Intermediate.***

*Sign Here*

X____________

Stanton was now sitting in an office type study with books and such everywhere. In front of him was an ornately carved desk that looked very old. In front of him was his cup of tea and the form.

"I love a good cup of tea, when I was a boy here in Russia my Oma, would have tea and gebäck. The world was very much colder then the teas would warm me through and through." his bony hands touched his cup rubbing the sides like it was warming his cold bony hands.

"You can sign that please, it is just a formality." pushing a very old pen towards him.

He picked it up before he could sign the Head Master Spoke again, stopping him in mid air.

"That pen is very old it has emitted many students to this school, you are not the first to use that." He smiled a bony smile.

Reading it through and then again, Stanton coughed then started to scratch his name.

Stanton...Scribbled

As the last letter was written to sign his name a flame caught the words, it burned into the page and then the whole page caught on fire, smoke and fumes and then nothing.

Stanton looked stunned he backed away from the desk as soon as the fire exploded from not just the page but also the words.

The headmaster rolled his head back and laughed a triumphant laugh there was that Sherlock Holmes thing again, Stanton thought.

"That is priceless, you would not expect us to keep a form with your name on it would you, hey boy, we are spies after all." laughing that huge laugh again. "That is a little trick you will learn about, we used to just burn the paper but sometimes if you where in a hurry there would be information still left on it."

# THE SCHOOL OF THE *CLOAKED KNIFE*

## CHAPTER 8

I am Felix Dzerzhinsky, you have figured out yes I am the headmaster here and Felix is what you will call me."

"What must I do now sir this is all rather much for me, I mean Felix." Stanton asked.

"You are to go down the hall, Miss Truancy will help you with your enrollment things. Each student has a uniform, a Surreptitious Entry Kit, a knife with an invisible sheath, a ring, and a first year pendant." continuing he said "Do not enter any other door, the second door on the left of you when you turn right, there is a door. On the door is a 2 in Russian and a gold seal underneath you cannot miss it."

Sitting down Felix went back to some papers on his desk and he did not speak again, this was Stanton's sign to leave the man here and move onto the next room.

Silently he closed the door behind him without saying anything he turned right and looked left yes there was the door with the seal on it.

Knocking before he entered, the door creaked slightly making it pretty obvious someone was opening the door.

It was a very clean office with a desk, with the usual things a typewriter, a telephone, a stapler, pens and pencil tin. There are some flowers on one corner and statue of a hammer and the sign for youth. Sitting behind the desk was an older women with gray hair, her beauty and elegance could still be seen through the withered lines and pale white skin.

"Ah young man, I have been waiting for you, Stanton right?"

"Yes ma'am" Stanton replied in his 12 year old voice.

"Sit dear, I have your box of things over here just give me a moment."

Setting the black box on the desk in front of him she doubled checked everything in the box and then picked it up and handed it to him.

She walked behind the desk and proceeded to push a big red button on the top of the desk by the phone. In a moment a skinny boy came through the door, his uniform was of a blue color and he looked different than the boys he had seen before.

"This is Timmins, he will help you make your way to your locker and the exit, you have seen enough for one day, you should be on your way back home before someone notices dear, come back tomorrow morning at the spot you are put out onto. Timmins will be waiting to take you to your orientation." she sat, putting her glasses back on that had just been resting on her chest from a golden rope that held them there.

"Come on." Timmins said as he opened and entered through another door at the back of the office.

They walked down a long corridor so black the floor and walls looked like glass; there was not a fingerprint anywhere, the floors and walls where spotless.

Walking through another door, they entered into a room like a gymnasium locker room

Lockers lined the walls everywhere and rows in between.

“You are locker 327.12 MEL” Timmins continued as he turned to leave, You are to go through that door, walk down to the front of the building, there will be a open door for you, that will lead you onto the street entrance. Look both ways when leaving make sure there is not a person staring or you will find yourself in the luuu.(Toilet), he continued again. “Be at the exact same spot tomorrow at 8 am, for your orientation, if you do not return this entrance will not be there for you again.”

Spinning on his heels Timmins left Stanton to his locker.

With a pounding heart Stanton opened the box peering inside his eyes opened wide with the collection of things he was just given.

*Orientation Spy list*

•Seal-Official S.O.C.K. pendant or badge

•Knife with Seal-Official S.O.C.K. knife with invisible sheath

•Uniform-Official S.O.C.K. garbs to be worn at all times in School

•Spy Handbook-Official S.O.C.K. rules book

•CipherDisk-Official S.O.C.K. code writer/breaker

•Code Paper and Holder-Walnut Code, Peanut Code and Coconut Code, the peanut was inside the walnut. *(The Walnut and the peanut where inside the Coconut like a Russian Babushka doll.)*

•Lock-Picking Kit-Leather pouch with a Feeler Pick, Half Diamond Pick, Rake, Reamer, Ball Rake, Broken-Key Removal Tool, Double Ball Rake, Double-Sided Tension Wrench

•Saw Kit-Plastic case with a Reamer, Saw Blade, Cutting Blade, Grinding Tool, Drill bit and a File

•Spy Kit-Leather pouch with a stick of gum, fishing line, a hook,(etc. invent more)

•Spy Level 1 School Book

•Sherlock Holmes Theory Book

•Map Reading Book

*S.O.C.K. Director of School*

*Headmaster*

Felix Dzerzhinsky

Felix Dzerzhinsky

**THE SCHOOL**
OF THE
***CLOAKED KNIFE***

# THE SCHOOL OF THE CLOAKED KNIFE

## CHAPTER 9

Taking each item out one by one Stanton tried to examine everything he was given but there was so much in the box. Stanton entirely did not know what all the stuff was. He pulled out the uniform examining the front. He put it on the hanger provided for him. There where places for everything in his locker and he did not find it difficult to put things in its place.

Closing the door he turned and left the locker room entering the open door he was told to enter.

There was a funny looking statue and a bunch of plants by the wall.

There was a walk-way that led downward, he now knew where he was it was the Bio-Sphere Pavilion a place where they grew plants in doors.

He walked into the open forest of plants and through a path, looking behind him he saw that the door was actually the wall that was painted and disguised as a portrait of a huge tree.

Looking around there was not a soul and from this angle you could tell there was not a person that could really see where he just came from it was hidden so well it was just a portrait of its surroundings.

The feeling of the tropical air inside the Bio-Sphere Pavilion made him feel chipper he was to become a Spy, he thought, me a Spy.

Skipping his feet he started humming a tune as he picked up his pace into a run, his energy souring inside him, he ran all the way home, the tide at his back he opened the door to his home, the smell of the chicken that was cooked that day was still in the air.

"Ah my little chicka dee, miss Stilton said what has such a lovely boy been up to this afternoon."

"He now remembered forgetting his book.

"I just read by the sea today and picked through the shells, not much,

lying with such a proud straight voice he felt like he was a spy.

His excitement was boiling inside him, he had taken the Pendant it poked his leg from inside his pants pocket. He fingered it as he turned to go to his room almost running but trying to keep his calm.

"20 minutes till Dinner, go wash yourself up before dinner."

"Okay" Stanton replied.

The next day he woke to the sun full and warm it made the sea shimmer in the morning so bright it blinded the onlooker. Stanton was skipping his feet, the pendant in his warm hand, the cold metal now hot from being inside his hand. Following the street, its winding way to the Bio-Sphere Pavilion to the spot where he was told to go. There was that thought of being too early. What was he to do? He could not just stand in that spot making himself known to every person. His 12-year-old mind was now going into fantasy mode, he imagined someone was following him. He stopped by a sign and looked up, pretending to read the sign but looking behind. They do not notice me he thought, he continued down the street, picking a different way he went onto the next street, now he stooped and went to tie his shoe. Looking behind him he once again pretended the pursuer was behind him. Running across the street he went around the long circle that led back to the front of the Bio-Sphere Pavilion building. He went to the door and walked in, looking behind him and to the left and right, good I have lost him he thought. The ramp led up to the other side where he needed to be looking again. He saw that Timmins was sitting and watching for him, he was not in uniform he was dressed in normal clothes. "Good Morning, Stanton, you are on time good, we are to go this way, I will lead you to the auditorium."

# THE SCHOOL OF THE CLOAKED KNIFE

## CHAPTER 10

They walked through the bushes that were just behind the bench and there was another path of dirt that led inside the huge forest. They walked to a fountain with lots of shiny coins in it.

This is called the Entrance of Wishes the entrance to the School is just behind that fountain.” Timmins said to Stanton.

“Most people will think that this is the office of lawyers as you can see it says “Law Offices” pointing to the door. Markings Underneath in Russian “===== ---------=====---==-=--=-==-=-=-=-.”

Pushing the door it went in and not out, like a swing door, you would think that there was more security.

“The most obvious is always the least observed.” Timmins said.

A security staff stood by the receptionist who sat in a circle of desks. On the wall there was a plaque with that insignia of the ring on it. A giant sign saying S.O.C.K. was on the wall as well as a circular lighting stage made the words of S.O.C.K. light up from behind the letters.

There was a picture of Felix behind the receptionist. He was wearing many medals and his special agent suit.

“Ah Timmins, where you to not finish the list of tasks I left for you last night.”

“Timmins face turned red.” but stayed silent

“You are to go to your locker Stanton put on your uniform and report to Room 113, do not take long, we must begin soon.” Timmins led Stanton to the locker room, waiting for Stanton to change.

“Leave all the rest of the stuff you will not need any of that now.”

Room 113 was full of students his age. They all sat at desks with low chairs, the wood was very old on the desks and gravity was evident from former students.

Scribbled on his was a picture of an ass of a donkey the caption underneath was in Russian.

Stanton laughed a quiet laugh and looked around, coughing he sat and stared blankly foreword.

A very rat like person crept into the classroom from the door that Stanton had entered. He walked silent and very catlike or I should say rat like. His beady face was captured underneath a pair of steel rim glasses that where perfectly round and almost to small for his face. His hands where very wrinkled but they seemed very precision like as he put down his book, pen and other papers he was carrying.

Tap Tap Tap

“Attention.”

Scratch Scratch Scratch his chalk was like steel on steel, the silence of the room was deafening to Stanton that chalk pierced his head, he did not like that about school, the noises the buzzing of the classes voice, too many things rushing past him, the fear that he might miss something or the thought that he should be doing something to remember it all. This always made him tired and a bit dizzy, his 12 year old mind working overtime, but this was different he seemed to have a purpose he was aching to see what the teacher had to show him.

Scratch Scratch Scratch the letters went down onto the chalk board.

"Mr. Wrinkler T. Walker"

"First Level S.O.C.K. Test"

He now stood looking at the entire class looking over top of his rimmed glasses his eyes serious and scouring like sand paper taking in every one like they where an open book.

"You!" He pointed at a small boy to the left of Stanton, "You have asthma, you are left handed, your favorite condiment is Ketchup (in Russian), and your name would be Yorky Scarsosky." not waiting for an answer he turned to another boy behind Stanton.

"You there!" he pointed at the taller boy in the class. "Your nationality is Czech, you have a limp obvious bicycle injury, and you have not changed your shirt for awhile so I gather you do not have a mother."

Once again not waiting for an answer Mr.Walker walked around the outer rim of the classroom, continuing to stared down everyone.

"You will see observation can give you many clues to the nature of any person."

"We must clearly define what we are seeing though, don't we, or the wrong information will give us the wrong observation."

"Raise of hands of those who knew that I was not of this country, my nationality is hidden to most of you I bet , my Russian is very good, speaking rapidly in Russian (=---)."

"Who can guess?"

# THE SCHOOL OF THE CLOAKED KNIFE

## CHAPTER 11

The tall boy who was called on instantly put his hand up.

"Yes boy, what is your answer."

"Americana, Teacher."

"How did you arrive at that."

"Your name on the board sir, you wrote it in English and the Name Walker I think is American."

"Good Job" Mr.Walker spoke and then continued, "You will be here again tomorrow morning. For now, you must move onto the gymnasium for calisthenics. Now go, I will see you all tomorrow."

The class moved out towards the gymnasium, Stanton followed still in wonder of the things to come. There was much to overcome for a 12 year old boy he. Stanton tripped into someone on his way out.

"Sorry" he said.

"That's ok I am Botzerki, your name is"

"Stanton?"

"Canadian."

"Oh."

"I have never met, Canadian, he spoke the name in a funny manner, like he had never said the word before."

"Those are my mates, Curtz and Mirzeke."Bozterki pointed to two boys standing waiting for him.

"You coming Botz."

"Ya let's go"

"We don't want to be in the front, hurry."

"Let's go Stanton." Botzerki spoke in his accented slowness.

The callisthenic session was grueling and Stanton almost damn near passed out from the squat thrusts. There was a new sense of purpose for him here now, the summer that was not going to be boring, alone to his thoughts, his parents off somewhere enjoying there usual adventure.

Once the session in the gym was over, and Stanton showered and re-uniformed ,he was now sitting in a peculiar shaped room that smelled of old wood and chalk dust. There was an uncomfortable creak that sounded from every one of the old chairs that him and the other students sat on. You could not quite find a comfortable place to sit and made you want to slouch down with your back against the backrest. The wood was so smooth on the chairs that the seat of Stanton's pants wanted him to slide forward, making it very uncomfortable.

"I am Stringent Zerkov, you can call me "Agent 53", I am to teach you the Basics of Tactical Weaponry and Spy-enty.

We will be going out into the yard today, there is to be a lesson in Proper Posture, Silent

Tracking, and my favorite, "The Cover Up, Tracing Forward and Walking Backwards."

The teacher handed leaflets to the farthest girl.

"Hand these out, pass them behind you."

"Roll call,"

Everyone accounted for, the teacher or Agent 53 Rather, went on to explain every letter they are given cannot pass the doors of the School, or it will spontaneous combust, there is to be no copying of files, and discussion of these matters will not leave the walls and the mind of the young pupil."

The lesson was elaborate and Stanton was so enthralled, there was a constant vision inside his head as Agent 53 talked. The afternoon was spent in the classroom; the teacher put many diagrams up onto the screen from a projector that was at the other end of the room. A boy of great size and shape was changing the images through the lesson that Agent 53 taught.

Finally the lesson was over and they where instructed to move to the courtyard just inside the compound, you would not have known this to exist from the outside the building looked like any other building in the industrial area that was behind the bio-gardens.

Passing a statue of Lennon, there was also a seal on the wall just behind the statue Stanton's keen 12-year-old mind, thought "I will come back and have a look at that"

Noticing that the class was held up at a giant door that led out into the courtyard and field, he decided to investigate that curious seal now instead of later.

Looking around to make sure that no one was looking, Stanton shifted on his heels and turned around.

Silently he went to the statue that was twice the size of him and there was a space that fit him.

Sliding in behind it, he was invisible now to anyone that approached.

# THE SCHOOL OF THE *CLOAKED KNIFE*

## CHAPTER 12

"Weird" He thought, "I feel a draft coming from somewhere." Stanton said to himself.

Moving his hand up and down against the wall he felt a draft, just slightly there was a hair line crack that outlined a door."

"I wonder how it is opened."

Searching around pushing on the door he now could see, it did not budge. Feeling the wall towards the seal, he stared at it.

"That is that peculiar symbol, on Felix's lapel"

He thought.

He heard the boys behind him making noises to move and the sound of the giant door creaking open. A gust of wind raced down the long hall past where Stanton stood.

Tracing his fingers over the curious seal. He felt its cold metal jutting out, its 3 dimensional patterns detected under his touch. Pushing hard onto the seal, it moved forward, a button rose out of the floor just below and near his left foot. Stepping on it there was a distant.

"Click"

The door in the wall slid open, revealing a dark entrance and a passage beyond.

Stepping through, the door again, slid behind him and a dim glow of light began to form from old frosted dirty bulbs that lined the passage in a consecutive order.

Stanton was a little scared at this point. He didn't really know where it led, but he pressed on.

The passage led to a T, one way led to a grate that looked like it might go to the outside,

the other way went to the right.

Walking to the grate, he looked outside, in the distance he could see his class, lining up against the trees, another hidden pathway led to the trees beside them.

"I better get back" He thought. "I can explore this later."

Pushing the grate open it sounded with a rusty screech, a few bows of trees had overgrown through it, and they sounded with a swift "Snap".

The path led through what looked like a bush that was impassable but somehow some one had built a path in between them that was hidden from either side.

It did not take him long to find a position that was right behind the class, crawling on all fours he managed to find his way through the thick bush. Standing up quick he stood beside the nearest student, a small, quiet, homely girl who was close to the woods. He crossed his arms, stood there and posed as if he were there the whole time.

The frail girl gazed at Stanton with a look of bewilderment, she was sure she was the only one standing at the back, she always stood at the back, she did not feel comfortable unless she was the last person, but said nothing and turned back to the teacher.

The last part of the day was the lessons of tracking, the lessons of evasion, and the lessons of proper walking techniques.

There was some humor from a few students that walked like ducks, they looked out of place, and you could hear the whispers from the others.

"That one is too fat, how is he to walk softly,"

Laughter erupted.

"Look at that tall one, he is lanky and towers over us how is he to walk softly." Laughter erupts again.

Stanton's turn he was to walk the course without making a footprint in either the grass or the dirt road that was the track that ran around in a circle.

"You must be calm and collected. Focus on your weight, imagine that you are weightless and our steps are above the ground." Agent 59 coached Stanton.

Bending forward slightly Stanton edges his way around the Silent Course. With his feet softly gliding along, he almost looked like a cat, except with precision he never knew he had.

"Good, good, a bit heavy over on the left side." Agent 59 said calling out loudly.

Stanton made it around the course in due time, the last of it was to cross a path of muddy ground You were to find a way to cross without leaving an impression that a person walked through here. The most difficult task since mud sticks to your boots and leaves any pressure points that you cannot hide.

Thinking quickly Stanton swirled his feet in a wide fashion creating a non descriptive pattern that seemed to settle back into itself leaving no foot print what so ever.

# THE SCHOOL OF THE CLOAKED KNIFE

## CHAPTER 13

"Well done, lad." Agent 59 came over to him clapped him on the back with a bony hand.

"You will do just fine here, we will go inside now class, for our day is almost done, there is one more task we must ask of you."

Their muddy boots where left at the door, and magically when they got back there was not a speck of mud on them. There were tables that lined one wall. On the tables were boxes of cereal, a pinwheel type of thing, the one from Stanton's spy kit was sitting in front.

"You will see that there is a box of cereal before all of you."

"This box will be your source of connection to us once you leave this school."

You are to purchase a box of this cereal from your nearest local grocer, there will be coded message on the back of the box, this message will keep you in contact of your obligations to this school." he continued "You will be trained in the art of de-coding and will understand what the wheel means in due time.

The wheel as you see becomes part of your book, you will find in your handbook a hidden compartment that will house it for you, do not let anyone else see you use this, keep it close."

A tall women with gray hair, high cheekbones and a

long skinny neck came into the room, her uniform was red with the symbol of the school on the lapel.

"This is Miss Kerkov, she will be your de-coding teacher, you will report to her tomorrow morning, for your next lessons. Exit with caution students, for that is your first task. Never get caught leaving this School, for that is instant expulsion!"

It was 12 to 1, the clock on the wall was in Russian but Stanton could guess what time it was by the silver knifes that represented the clock pointers. There was a dull hum in the air that came from the florescent lights that hung from above his head, their dim light filling the corners with shadows and darkness.

The seat of the teacher was creaking, and the test in front of him was making his head swim.

The question "What is the nearest sound that you would hear if there was bird in the tree to the south, a train whistle to the west, the sound of a women's voice behind you and the sound of cars to the rear of you?"

He thought for a long moment and then without a flinch he wrote "My Feet"

The test said at the top "Test One Entry Level"

The clock seemed to not move at all, even at the question number 20; he flicked the rest of the papers with his fingers and sighed. He really detested these things; there was always that anxiety he had about picking the right question.

"Should I just pick C," he thought.

Twenty minutes passed and he was finally getting to the last question.

"Tap, Tap, Tap."

"Ok put your pencils down"

"You will wonder, why this test?"

"It is a placement test, your knowledge will help us find a place for you in our school, and everyone will be assigned a sector." She pulled at her sleeves and adjusted her dress.

"Put the test face down on the desk and we will see you all tomorrow."

# THE SCHOOL OF THE *CLOAKED KNIFE*

## CHAPTER 14

Stanton lay upon his bed with his feet hanging over the edge, his socks just barely on. His mind was a sunder of thoughts.

"Where shall they put me? Am I to be a special agent, a bomb specialist, a 'Bug', A Snitch, or maybe a 'Stincher.'"

Stincher being the loneliest of spies, and was to stay locked in an attic or room, spending their time collecting information.

"Come for dinner, Stanton."

"I have Chicken Pot Pies and your favorite warmed apples and caramel sauce with cold cream for desert. Quick! Come before the pie gets cold, hurry dear, you should wash your hands."

Stanton came down to the kitchen and began eating, always with his eyes on the plate.

He was not drawing attention to the scratch that he had on the back of his neck. The scratch that now ached with a throbbing nag, the kind of nag that you have to scratch, scratching the scratch made it bleed and now he was sure she could notice his discomfort.

"You have been such a busy bee, what could take your attention so early in the morning."

"I guess when I was your age I was out at the break of dawn, finding adventure about the day."

Stanton munched more of the inside of the Chicken

Pot Pie, it was very good the gravy seeping around his spoon, he let it slide onto his tongue.

She would talk most of the time, not even noticing he was not answering.

"Well you must have something very adventurous planned, indeed? Oh dear I must be old to you."

She straightened her hair and wiped her cheeks with the back of her hand.

"When I was a small girl, I was a looker, I tell you, the boys would try to walk me home and hold my books."

"Do you like your pie dear."

Stanton nodded as he slipped the last piece of crust with the gravy into his mouth.

"I have not talked with your Parents but they are to call tomorrow, you should make sure you are close, I don't want to yell my voice thin calling your name.

"You are to have a bath tonight young man, all that adventuring makes for a dirty 12 year old boy.

"Desert now Dear." she spoke again not waiting for an answer she went to spooning out the warmed apples. A giant scoop of cold cream made thicker by the whisk she was just removing from the bowl.

"Off with you now" as he licked the spoon clean.

"Don't forget behind your ears."

"Come give us a hug."

Stanton escaped the never-ending voice of Miss Sheldon he could hear her now singing under her voice as she went to do the dishes.

The night was dark as he slipped into his bed, cold at first then warmed by his body. The mind of a 12 year old went into the reflection of what had just transpired that day. The placement test was to be discussed tomorrow he was to find out his position and place in S.O.C.K. There was also a mission status report to fill out and his first mission was to be posted on the wall tomorrow. He was to meet his fellow sector members.Toobtainhisbadgeandrankhewastold,thefirst mission must be completed in the first 24 hours or he was to be held back until the next session. There was only one spot and one spot only. He was nervous but he knew he could complete the mission and he was excited. Pulling the covers up over his head he closed his eyes.

## Epilogue

As Stanton drifted off to sleep he was imagining the adventure he was going to have. Tomorrow was his first day at the school and his first mission. All Stanton could think about was that he was now a real spy. His thoughts drifted as his eyes closed and he fell deep asleep to the echoing of his own voice.

"I am to be a spy he said."

"A spy."

## Conclusion

This ends the first pilot story of S.O.C.K., *The School Of The Cloaked Knife*. Stay tuned as the book continues in a full-length novel. Stanton becomes familiar with the school and bonds with his new found friends. A dark mystery is discovered as Stanton becomes trapped within a cat and mouse game with an unknown assailant.

*Stay Tuned…*

## *A Note From The Author*

While working on the sequel to S.O.C.K., another story began to weave itself with in my mind. I decided to give readers a preview of my next novel *"The Endless Ruins Of Time"* by sharing the short story that has evolved into the first full-length novel of my life.

# The Old Tree

*Story Written By Garry Turner*

*Taken from The Endless Ruins Of Time...*

The Branch from a very old and winding tree, its old knotted bark showing its age as much as its size scraped along the window. The wind whistling shaking the leaves as the branch moved back and fort, scraping its message over and over against the window, that creepy constant rhythm of bang-bang, scrape-scrape, rustle and shake. Something a young boy never really forgets about when alone, it is always that sound that keeps a young mind full of imagination and anticipation. Shadows in the dark, a pair of eyes staring from the closet and the always "looming beast" under the bed and many other conjured up visions of sound and wonder. This particular old tree is every kid's dream right by the window, with easy access to the ground below and easy access to the roof above. Its large limbs easy to climb and its spacious and large sized made it a mark for building the perfect Tree house, but for this particular boy Roddy it was a kid's nightmare it scared him. Its old and gnarly bark and the scraping and whistling would send him shivering under his covers on many nights.

Roddy Swartz was an average kid of average height,

average build, with an average IQ and in general just a normal average everyday kid. His 12 Years Old stature and being the only 12 Year Old historian around has brought him to believe himself as Broken Rivers very own Historical Society. Broken River being the town Roddy and his family had moved to after a great Uncle mysterious disappearance and the old estate was offered to them in his will. Great Uncle Swartz was a very old eccentric, collector of antiquities and archeology.

Roddy had only met his Uncle once at the age of ten and he had left no lasting impression on Roddy. The only thing Roddy had which he was allowed to keep was an old Calvary hat and a picture of his Uncle under the tree reading a very large book. The look on his Uncle's face always made him stare at the picture for hours. It was the look of complete amazement and wonder, whatever the book entailed had to be magic with his Uncle's eye's on fire with that look of amazement. Once again the old tree outside speaks its furious tone, bang-bang, scrape- scrape rustle and shake. Roddy hated Halloween people out scaring one another for candy what a ridiculous ritual he thought to himself as he looked outside past the old tree. He could see it was just getting dark. The Weather was warm and mild but you could feel the October storm brewing in the air, the wind whistling picking up stronger, making the old tree speak even more bang-bang, scrape-scrape, rustle and shake.

Roddy shivered from the sound going all the way up his spine goose bumps forming on his arms. Roddy really tried not to think about the old tree as his eyes went back to the map of the Broken River Museum. He was trying to remember where he could have left his notebook. Since Roddy was just an average boy he always ended up having an average problem of always leaving his notebook somewhere. On purpose his parents and teacher had said to him many times not to leave his notebook lying around. This time he was really trying to remember where he had left it before it was too late and once again he would have to stay after school and catch up on last weeks assignments. His teacher Professor Stilt said to him he would lose his head if it where not screwed on properly. Even as loosely as it was screwed on you seem to find ways to lose your notebook. Then Professor Stilt would roll his eyes and hold his hands up and shrug his shoulders with a loud gasp. One of these days "Roddy" you might surprise us and forget to put your pants on before you get to school laughing as he did with that teacher chalk board laugh stiff and direct. Trying to ignore the sounds coming from the side of the house. The big tree scraping against the window, bang-bang, scrape-scrape, rustle and shake.

Roddy studied the map.

Saying to the air.

"Well I started at the giant collection of Indian spear

heads like I always do".

"Where would I have had time to put my notebook down." He repeated to the empty room.

Bang-bang, scrape-scrape, rustle and shake BANG-BANG the old tree spoke furiously this time, making him put down the museum map. Roddy went to the window and looked outside there was a storm brewing its center could be seen in the distance a dark looming cloud. Thunder sounding in the distance a small fragment of a lightning bolt poking from the clouds dark center. The wind was really picking up he thought glad I am not one of those poor wretches that are out tricking for candy. He would sneak a nickel out of jar on top of the fridge once in a while and go to Harry's Garage. The store was a bike ride away and he liked Harry. Harry had a nickel machine with giant gumballs in it. You know the ones that are too big for your mouth and you had to really try hard to chew one all at once they where so big. If Roddy got a green one harry would give him one for free. Sometimes he would clean the oil stained floor and harry would let him read the newspaper "The Daily Forecast" the local newspaper. Always on Saturday they had a special comics section with his favorite comic strips.

Roddy would always read the obituary section and strange news section. Sometimes they would have stories of UFO sighting and other strange news. One particular story was very interesting to Roddy it was about an unusual artifact found very close to his family's estate it made front page news and the whole town took the museum tour to have a look at it. That is what really started all the trouble with his missing notebook. Roddy had gone to see the artifact in the newspaper without his parents knowing of course. Sneaking in and then losing his notebook would really not go over to well. Shaking his head he whispered under his breath.

"You will lose your head if wasn't screwed on right."

Imitating Professor Stilts laugh to a "T" even Roddy made himself cringe by the sound. Bang-bang, scrape-scrape rustle and shake the old tree again resounded with its torment.

"Damn that storm is brewing" saying it out loud to himself.

"That storm is really ugly" repeating the words somehow was comforting Roddy.

He looked around the room the shadows dancing on the ceiling.

The shadows reached the far corners under his bed and into the back of the closet. He looked into the closet with a shiver he stood up. Roddy went over to his closet and closed the doors best not think about any of that he told himself. He went to sit back down standing for a moment he stared at the museum map sitting at his desk. Bang and then a crash the window resounded with a mighty thud. Another thud against the wall the wind and then the window flew open the wind whistling around the room. The map flew off the table and the chair blew over onto the floor. The wind blew heavily and the rain poured in through the window. Roddy pushed the window closed with a sounding "Click" the window locked firmly. The wind continued to howl outside and the tree shook against the window.

Picking the map up off the floor he noticed something on the map he never noticed before on the back of the pamphlet. There was a small picture of what seemed to be his Uncle with two other people. They seemed to be all looking at something his Uncle was holding. The main part of the picture is the huge Museum sign. It was to be the same but the surrounding where not at all the same in the picture. He stared at the picture again this cannot be astounded he kept looking.

"Okay" he said. "This is strange, there was no trees under the sign at the Broken River Museum." Roddy's voice was excited. He was sure of that.

Roddy also knew that there never was a fountain like that in front of the gates of the Broken River Museum. As far as he could remember from old newspaper clippings in the library everything in this pictures was wrong. 7676 Horgrath St. was just barely noticeable under the big Broken River Museum sign, which in the photo was hidden by large trees. This really had his interest now because there was no such thing as Horgrath St. in Broken River. Being the town's historian he had been in every nook and cranny of this small little river community. This now made him think back to the picture of his Uncle Swartz. It was the picture of his Uncle that was hung up on a long piece of wire and a nail. Walking over to the wall he took it down and went back to his seat at the desk. Bang-bang, scrape-scrape, whistle, rustle and shake that sound came again still telling of the oncoming storm he shivered a bit and proceeded to look at the picture of his Uncle Swartz. He stared more closely at the book in his Uncle's hands. Nothing oh wait he could make out a few letters on the cover Ho...r...t...1506... I wonder what that means scratching his left side of his forehead just like he would always do when his thinking went to real hard thinking. The only things he new about his Uncle Swartz was the story's his Mother and Father had told him. Everyone else seemed to shy away from talking about his Uncle Swartz at all. He knew he was an anthropologist and was quite eccentric. The pictures and all the stuff his uncle collected had shown that eccentricity. The boars head in the study was quite nasty, that thing gives me the creeps he thought to himself the eyes seem to follow him when he would go in there. He was not allowed to touch any of the books in his uncle study, they where all under lock and key and know one seemed to know where it was. Asking time and time again he was demanded not to ask again or the leather strap would be used on his behind. This being a young boy was torture he often thought of picking the locks and stealing the books but he knew better of it. Just to get one look at one of those books he would just dream of that day. The library in Broken River seemed so boring to Roddy, how many more times he can take out The Hardy Boys, or the Belgariad Series. They only had one book on Sherlock Holmes and it was the "Hounds of the Baskervilles". Roddy could tell you the story backwards and forwards. Holmes solves the crime move on he thought.

They had two books on dinosaurs in the small library. Roddy's favorite dinosaur the Tyrannosaurus Rex was left out. He asked the librarian why and she had said it had been taken out of the books because it was too frightening to talk about. The only book on Native Indians(Aboriginals)was a pamphlet on the Indian Arrow Heads at the museum.

Roddy was still dreaming of the giant case of books in his uncle's study he could imagine the contents. He imagined stories and pictures of Inca gold, Viking treasure, Egyptian tombs and sacred scrolls. Bang-bang, scrape-scrape, whistle, rustle and shake. Suddenly thunder loud as the sky and as big as

Broken River erupted outside. The wind shaking the old tree outside made Roddy jump-his heart pounded as he heard the rain starting to pour smashing its hurried droplets onto the window making him shiver again. Then there was another thunderous boom, then a flash of lightning.

Boom-boom-boom.

Lightning Flashes.

Then all of a sudden an even bigger crash sounded and then a bolt of lightning strikes the old tree outside the window. Then with a thunderous clap the bolt as long as the sky bright as the biggest star sizzled the top of the old tree off with a bang and a creak it toppled to the ground. Roddy ran to the window and opened it with one quick motion.

BANG!"

He hit his head on the top of the frame as he opened the window.

"Ouuch" he yelled.

Looking outside to his amazement the top of the tree is on fire like a huge torch. What was the top of the tree now laid on the ground beneath it, crushed and crumpled smoking. There was a blurring sensation around Roddy. He felt it as sure as the sky was blue and the day turned into night. Roddy held onto the frame of the window as he felt like he was going to pass out. This sensation had happened to him a couple of times when he was a kid. Once was when he was playing at the park, he had just climbed the tallest rungs of the metal loops that twisted up from the ground. There was a flash off in the distance and then a big dark cloud had flown in above him. The sound of the thunder was loud and the lightening bolt struck near him. He held onto the metal beams scared as hell, wondering how and if he was ever going to get off the play bars. The blurring sound was around his ears just like that day, the day he passed out from that blurring sound and woke up on the wet ground covered in mud. It had happened a few times before and he knew to grab a hold of something and wait it out. There where voices that floated to his ears, he could here a voice speaking from somewhere into the blur that was his room.

*To be continued…*

www.ingramcontent.com/pod-product-compliance
Ingram Content Group UK Ltd.
Pitfield, Milton Keynes, MK11 3LW, UK
UKHW020218250726
13967UKWH00001B/75

9 781257 776122